Father Sun, Mother Moon

John and Ann Hassett

HOUGHTON MIFFLIN COMPANY BOSTON 2001

Walter Lorraine Books

For Mom

Walter Lorraine (WL) Books

Copyright © 2001 by John and Ann Hassett
All rights reserved. For information about permission
to reproduce selections from this book, write to
Permissions, Houghton Mifflin Company, 215 Park
Avenue South, New York, New York 10003.

Library of Congress Cataloging-in-Publication Data
Hassett, John
  Father Sun, Mother Moon / by John and Ann Hassett.
   p. cm.
  Summary: In a village where everything is painted white,
a stranger agrees to paint the school in order to avoid bad luck,
but instead teaches the villagers a valuable lesson.
  ISBN 0-395-97565-4
  [1. Superstition—Fiction. 2. Color—Fiction.] I. Hassett, Ann (Ann M.) II. Title.

PZ7.H2785 Fat 2001
[E]—dc21

                                     00-033609

Printed in the United States of America
WOZ 10 9 8 7 6 5 4 3 2 1

Father Sun, Mother Moon

Once a stranger came to a place where all things were painted white. "Our village has worn white paint for as long as the sun and moon have sailed the heavens," the villagers said. "If ever the village were not white, all the children would grow foolish."

The children stared at the stranger's clothes. "Once I found a rainbow tangled in a thorn tree," she told them. "I played my flute and the rainbow floated free. Father Sun was pleased, so he gave me clothes of the rainbow's colors."

As she spoke, a black cloud
appeared over the village.
Suddenly a bolt of lightning
flashed down upon the village
school. It turned the school to
gray. "Bad luck has found us!
All is not white. Soon the
children will grow foolish,"
cried the villagers.
"I will paint the school,"
the stranger said.

The next morning she sat atop the gray school playing the flute. Not once did she reach for her pots of paint.

"Father Sun likes to hear my flute as he wakes," she said to the children.
"As a favor he is painting the clouds for us."

"Father Sun likes to hear my flute when he has climbed highest in the sky," she said to the children. "As a favor he is painting the sea for us."

"The school still is not white," said the villagers. To bring good luck they stood on their heads.

"Father Sun likes to hear my flute before he sleeps," the stranger said to the children. "As a favor he is painting the hills for us." To bring good luck the villagers carried toads in their pockets.

The sun set over the hills, and the moon rose from the sea. Still the stranger sat atop the school that was not white. To bring good luck the villagers spoke backwards — "foolish grow will children Now," they whispered.

"Mother Moon also likes to hear my flute," the stranger said to the children. "Tonight she will grant us a favor." The stranger reached for her pots of paint.

She painted in the moonlight.
Word spread backwards from
house to house. "last at us found
luck Good," said the villagers
from their beds.

The moon drifted through the stars.

22

All that night the stranger painted.

23

Sleepy owls hooted from the cactus forest
while the moon dropped lower. Faster and
faster the stranger painted, till she brushed
a last stroke from the last pot of paint.

A rooster crowed.
As the villagers awoke they looked toward the school. "Now the children will not grow foolish!" they cheered. But as the moon set over the hills and the sun rose from the sea, a strange thing happened.

The school was not white at all. It was colored with yellow paint as bright as the sun. "Mother Moon has fooled us!" shouted the children. "Father Sun shows it is so."

After that day, the villagers painted all things with the colors of the rainbow. The stranger was never seen again. But on nights when the moon was full, the children could hear her flute. And, of course, they did not ever grow foolish.

END THE